DISNEY
fairies

*Lily*
*in Full*
*Bloom*

# Lily
## in Full
## Bloom

WRITTEN BY
LAURA DRISCOLL
& PAMELA BOBOWICZ

ILLUSTRATED BY
JUDITH HOLMES CLARKE, LOREN CONTRERAS
& ADRIENNE BROWN

RANDOM HOUSE 🏠 NEW YORK

*Library of Congress Cataloging-in-Publication Data*

Driscoll, Laura.

Lily in full bloom / written by Laura Driscoll & Pamela Bobowicz;
illustrated by Judith Holmes Clarke, Loren Contreras &
Adrienne Brown.

p.   cm.

Summary: Garden-talent fairy Lily invents a new kind of flower that she
names the panglory, and while the blooms start out as she expects, they
soon lose their color, along with all of the other plants in Pixie Hollow.

ISBN 978-0-7364-2608-4 (pbk.)

*[1. Flowers—Fiction. 2. Fairies—Fiction. 3. Gardening—Fiction.] I. Clarke,
Judith, ill. II. Contreras, Loren, ill. III. Brown, Adrienne, ill. IV. Title.*

PZ7.D79Lil 2010

[Fic]—dc22          2009026426

www.randomhouse.com/kids/disney

Printed in the United States of America

10 9 8 7 6 5 4 3 2 1

# All About Fairies

IF YOU HEAD toward the second star on your right and fly straight on till morning, you'll come to Never Land, a magical island where mermaids play and children never grow up.

When you arrive, you might hear something like the tinkling of little bells. Follow that sound and you'll find Pixie Hollow, the secret heart of Never Land.

A great old maple tree grows in Pixie

Hollow, and in it live hundreds of fairies and sparrow men. Some of them can do water magic, others can fly like the wind, and still others can speak to animals. You see, Pixie Hollow is the Never fairies' kingdom, and each fairy who lives there has a special, extraordinary talent.

Not far from the Home Tree, nestled in the branches of a hawthorn, is Mother Dove, the most magical creature of all. She sits on her egg, watching over the fairies, who in turn watch over her. For as long as Mother Dove's egg stays well and whole, no one in Never Land will ever grow old.

Once, Mother Dove's egg *was* broken. But we are not telling the story of the egg here. Now it is time for Lily's tale. . . .

Disney
fairies

Lily
in Full
Bloom

# 1

A LIGHT BREEZE whispered through the long grasses by the pond. It rustled the leaves of the Home Tree. It bent the stems of the primroses by the courtyard. It tickled the wings of fairies and sparrow men throughout Pixie Hollow. Everyone was busy and happy and hard at work.

Everyone, that is, except Lily, a garden-talent fairy. She was busy, but not so happy.

Lily was in her garden, which was one of the most beautiful spots in Pixie Hollow. Some fairies came there to relax on soft clover beds. Others came to smell the flowers—jasmine and lilacs and roses. Lily liked to sit and watch the grass grow.

But today, she was crouched next to a bare patch of sandy soil. She was carefully digging out a drooping plant. Its leaves were brown and wilted.

Lily frowned. She knew some plants needed extra love and attention to grow strong. But this was the fourth time she had tried to plant in this patch of her garden. And the fourth time she had failed.

By her side, Lily had a pot ready with fresh soil. She placed the droopy roots deep into the dirt and patted down around the stalk. More than anything, she hated to see a plant that didn't know where to bloom.

Lily stared down at the bare patch. She was completely stumped. "If only I could get something to grow here," she muttered.

The soil was sandy—not the best type for most plants. Lily had tried fruits and herbs and two different kinds of flowers. But none of them had taken root. Still, she didn't want to give up yet.

She stepped out of her corn-husk slippers and dug her toes into the sandy soil. Maybe if she could feel what the soil felt, she could figure out which plant might have a chance of growing in this patch. Something that liked dry soil, such as sage or rosemary? Maybe a hardy flower, like a black-eyed Susan?

Lily's bee friend Bumble buzzed over while Lily worked. She was concentrating very hard and barely noticed him. It wasn't until he'd buzzed around her head twice that she finally looked up.

"Bumble!" she said. "When did you get here?" Bumble dove into a flower and Lily's thoughts returned to her problem.

"What am I going to do about this spot?" she asked.

Bumble popped out of one poppy and dove into another. As Lily watched her friend, her stomach rumbled. Her garden had kept her so busy that she'd forgotten about teatime!

Lily wasn't normally one to trade time in her garden for chitchat over tea. But that afternoon, a short break was just what she needed. Maybe Iris or Rosetta or one of the other garden talents would know what to do with her problem patch.

She hopped out of the sandy soil

and put her slippers back on. Then she left her tools in her garden shed, rinsed her hands, and fluttered off toward the Home Tree.

When Lily got to the tearoom, most of the fairies and sparrow men already were seated. She felt an unusual energy in the room. She grabbed a slice of cake and slid into a seat next to Rosetta.

"What's going on?" Lily whispered.

"Lily!" Rosetta exclaimed. "Have you heard the news?"

"What news?" Lily asked. "I just got here. There's a problem patch in my garden that—"

"Did you hear?" Iris interrupted. She flew between her two friends. "Tinker Bell has a new invention."

"An invention?" Lily looked at the pots-and-pans table across the room. All the tinkers were out of their seats and crowded around Tinker Bell. Fairies from other talent groups also hovered nearby.

Pots-and-pans fairies were known for creating new and useful things out of the scraps in their workshops.

"It sure must be fascinating!" said Iris. She flew over to the tinkers' table to get a better view. Lily, Rosetta, and the other garden talents followed.

Peeking between fairies' wings, Lily saw an odd-looking hat on Tink's head. It looked like it had been hammered out from an old teapot. Clipped to the front was a small, round mirror.

The crowd pressed in closer as more and more fairies came to see Tink's invention. "What's the hat for?" Lily heard the fairy next to her ask.

"Fawn," Tink called out. When Tink spotted the animal-talent fairy, she waved her closer. "Can you ask a firefly to help me?"

"I'll get Glowyn," Fawn said. She put two fingers in her mouth and let out an earsplitting whistle.

Before Lily could blink, a firefly zipped through a window to Fawn's side. A quick word from Fawn, and Glowyn perched on the hat's brim. Tink made sure the hat was settled correctly on her head and then nodded to Fawn.

Fawn whispered to Glowyn, and

suddenly, his tail flared brightly. His glow reflected off the hat's mirror. A strong beam of light shot out from Tink's hat and lit up the room.

The crowd gasped. The fairies at the front of the group shaded their eyes with their hands. The light was so bright!

"It's a firefly-headlamp hat!" Tink said proudly. "It's for moonless nights. Or anytime when your glow is not quite strong enough to fly by. All you need is this hat and a friendly firefly."

Applause filled the room. The pots-and-pans fairies cheered the loudest. The other talents offered their congratulations to Tink as well.

"Great idea, Tink!" exclaimed Rani, a water-talent fairy.

"Amazing!" agreed Lympia, a laundry fairy.

"That's so practical!" cried Fira. As a light talent, she worked extra hard on moonless nights. A hat like this might make her job easier.

Tink turned to smile at her friends. As she did, the light hit several fairies right in the eyes. Each blinked and looked away.

"Oops," said Tink. She took off the hat and set it on the table. Fawn said something to Glowyn in Firefly language, and he flew off through the window.

The fairies and sparrow men crowded in even closer to get a good look at the hat. Tink was peppered with questions about her new invention.

"How did you think of it?" Fawn wanted to know.

"How soon can we get one?" Rani and Silvermist asked at the same time.

"Is the beam brighter than a light talent's glow?" Fira wondered aloud.

"Will there be one for everyone?" Terence, a fairy-dust sparrow man, asked.

Tink held up a hand. "Hold on," she said. "This is just a sample. It'll be a while before I have more hats. The tinkers are pretty busy these days."

Aster chuckled. "Yeah, I guess we're all pretty busy. I spend so much time in my garden I sometimes forget to eat!"

Many of the fairies and sparrow men, including Lily, nodded in agreement. Aster had said just what Lily was thinking. They started to talk about their work piling up on their tables.

Lily leaned over to Rosetta and whispered, "I've got a problem patch in my garden. I could use your advice about it if you have time."

But before Rosetta could respond, Tink's voice rang out. "I'm sure you're all busy, too," Tink said. "But it's the pots-and-pans talents' job to think up great ideas to help everyone!"

All the other fairies grew quiet. They looked at each other uncertainly.

Lily felt she had to speak up. "But Tink, every talent has great ideas."

"Of course," Tink said slowly. She tugged at her bangs. "It's just that . . . well, tinkers *tinker.* We invent. We make things from nothing. That's what we do. . . ."

Everyone stayed quiet. They stared at Tink and the other pots-and-pans fairies, who stood awkwardly behind her.

"That's true," Fira said. She crossed her arms. "But I'm sure we could *all* use our talents to invent things, too. You know, if we put our minds to it."

"I want to try!" Beck said. Her face was full of determination.

"Me too," Lympia chimed in.

"I bet we can all come up with something really great!" Fira said. "The light talents will have a dazzling idea, I'm sure!"

The energy from moments before had returned to the tearoom. All the fairies and sparrow men buzzed about what they could invent with their talents.

Lily's glow flared with excitement. She loved a challenge. She had never tried to invent anything before!

The crowd quickly broke apart. Rosetta and Iris fluttered back to the garden-talent table. They were already talking about their ideas. Lily trailed behind, deep in thought. Bits of ideas were swirling in her head.

And then one idea started to take shape. An idea that might help her garden, the other garden talents, and all of Pixie Hollow at the same time.

Lily knew it was a big idea and that it would take a lot of work. But if she could figure out all the small details . . .

## 2

LILY SPENT THE NEXT two days stretched out on a patch of soft moss in her garden, gazing at her pansies. The other fairies must have thought she was resting. Or relaxing. Or maybe even napping. But she wasn't doing any of those things.

She was, in fact, hard at work. Pansy-watching was the best way of doing research for her invention idea.

Which pansies grew best, and why? Exactly what did each flower need? Lily went over it again and again. Finally, she had a plan.

On day three, Lily sprang into action. Bothered by her sudden movement, Bumble buzzed off to another flower patch in the farthest corner of the garden.

First, Lily gathered all the things she would need. She already had plenty of pansy seeds. But she also needed plant food. And water—lots of water.

She grabbed three toadstool watering cans and flew to the garden fairies' well. It was tucked away near a thicket of rosebushes a few minutes' flight from her

garden. The well was a popular spot for the garden fairies to gather. They came to fetch water, see their friends, and talk about any problem plants. But this morning, only Iris and Bluebell were there.

Bluebell was filling her watering can. Iris, as usual, was talking. Iris was the only garden fairy who didn't have a garden. Still, she knew more about plants than any other fairy in Pixie Hollow. She also knew everything that was going on in everyone else's garden— and was quick to offer advice.

But today Iris wasn't talking about gardening. She was talking about inventions. For the past three days, none of the fairies had talked about much else.

Lily dropped her watering cans next

to the well and waited for Bluebell to finish.

"Lily!" Iris cried. "Have you heard? The animal talents have a great idea for an invention. It's a hawk-repelling whistle! One blow makes a hawk want to get as far away as possible!"

Lily pulled up a bucket of water from the well. "It *is* a great idea," she said. "And it would make Pixie Hollow much safer. I hope they can get it to work."

Lily meant what she had said. She was a generous fairy, with a heart as big as a sunflower. She truly hoped that each talent would come up with an invention that would make them proud. But she also had a secret—the idea that she was working on. She wasn't ready to share it with Iris or Bluebell or any of the other garden fairies. Not until she was sure it would work. But she couldn't help wondering if her idea would impress Iris as much as the hawk whistle had.

When her three watering cans were filled, Lily returned to her garden. Her mind was swirling with thoughts.

She left her full watering cans by the garden shed. Then she flew over to the Home Tree. She needed one more thing for her invention.

On her way, Lily spotted Lympia, who was hanging the wash out to dry. Lympia saw Lily, too, and called her over.

"How are you coming along with invention ideas?" Lympia asked.

Lily didn't know how to answer. Her own idea wasn't ready to share yet. Maybe she could say that she was thinking hard about it.

"I have an idea," she admitted. "But it's not fully worked out." Lily saw a sparkle in Lympia's eyes. She sensed that Lympia wanted to be asked the same question. "And you?" she asked.

Lympia nodded excitedly. "I don't like to brag," she began, "but I mixed up this new kind of laundry cleaner yesterday. It whitens like nothing I've ever seen before!"

"Lympia, that's great!" Lily replied. "I have a pussy-willow shirt with blueberry stains all over it."

Lily was proud of her friend. Like

the hawk whistle the animal talents were working on, Lympia's laundry cleaner would help all of Pixie Hollow.

"This was such a great idea," Lympia said. "I'm so glad Tink came up with it."

"Me too," Lily said. Though she wondered if *Tink* was glad she'd come up with the idea. She had a feeling Tink would have been happy to keep the inventing to herself!

"I'll let you know how my cleaner turns out," Lympia said. "And good luck with your idea, Lily. I can't wait to hear all about it!"

Lily waved good-bye and flew to the Home Tree kitchen. She thought more about her idea. As she ran the details over and over in her mind, she started to become more confident again. Just the thought of her invention made her smile.

When Lily got to the kitchen pantry, she went right to the spice racks. She knew the baking talents wouldn't mind if she borrowed some spices. She quickly found just what she was looking for. She put the spices into her woven-reed pouch and returned to her garden.

At her garden shed, Lily dropped off her pouch. She picked up an acorn bowl full of pansy seeds, her water-filled cans, and some fairy dust. She carried all her supplies to a shady spot under an apple tree and spread them out.

For the next hour, she mixed and watered and watered and mixed. She sprinkled lots of fairy dust into the

bowl. She closed her eyes and tried to listen to the seeds. Then she mixed and watered and mixed some more.

Between the mixing and the fairy dust, Iris landed at Lily's side. She chattered on about the water talents' new invention. Lily heard Iris say something about a singing fountain and a babbling brook. But Lily barely looked up from her seeds. She needed to focus on her own invention. Then she noticed that Iris had stopped talking. She was wringing her hands nervously.

"Iris?" Lily asked. She set down her tools and turned to face her friend.

"Oh, what are we going to do? All the other talents have great invention ideas. We've got nothing!" Iris said.

"Don't worry, Iris," Lily answered calmly. "We'll think of something."

" 'Think of something'? I'm not sure you understand. This is about garden-fairy pride!" Iris snapped. "Lily, you're smart. Can't you take a break from whatever it is you're doing with those seeds? I'm sure you could think up an invention for us. You discovered the Ever tree, after all!"

Without waiting for a reply, Iris flew off. Lily smiled. Iris had been so concerned about the other fairies' inventions that she hadn't even noticed what Lily was doing!

If everything went well, Iris would have nothing to worry about. Lily's seeds would become the most amazing plants in Pixie Hollow. All the care she was showering on them would pay off very soon.

## 3

FOR THE NEXT FEW DAYS, Lily thought about her invention every moment. It was even on her mind as she slept. The name for her new seeds had come to her while she was dreaming. "Panglories!" Lily cried. She sat bolt upright in her flower-canopied bed. "That's it! Glorious pansies! I'll call them *panglories!*"

Lily wrote the name on a scrap of leaf paper. Then she stretched her arms and yawned. The sky outside her window was the light gray of early dawn. It was much earlier than she usually got up. She lay in her bed, trying to go back to sleep. But she was too wound up.

She hopped out of bed. She put on her tunic and knickers and grabbed her sun hat. "It's time to see if those little seeds do what I hope they can!" she said with a shake of her wings. Then she quickly flew off to her garden.

The morning sun was peeking through the trees. Lily brought her gardening tools, the seeds, and her watering can to the bare patch of soil in the corner of her garden.

She pulled a green sea-glass bottle out of her pocket. Inside were her seeds. She held the bottle up to her eyes. She wanted to give the seeds one final pep talk before planting them.

"Okay, little seeds," she said. "Grow strong. Grow happy." Then she drew the bottle even closer and dropped her voice to a whisper. "I believe in you."

Lily tipped the bottle and a batch of seeds fell into her palm. She sprinkled them onto the sandy soil. Then she showered them with a generous helping of water.

Lily was too excited to sit still and wait. She flew this way and that. She paced and waited and wondered and hoped. She was usually very patient. But

today she was finding it hard to wait for her little seeds to bloom.

Lily needed to put her mind on something else. It was still on the early side, but there was a good chance she'd find someone who was awake now. Maybe time would pass more quickly if she could share her excitement.

She corked the bottle of seeds and slipped it back into her pocket. Then she flew to the Home Tree. She was half hoping to run into Tink. She'd like to tell her about her seeds.

But when she got to the lobby, it was empty. Lily paused for a minute, thinking of where to go next. Then Lympia zipped past. She was flying toward the laundry room with a pile of tablecloths in her arms.

"Lympia!" Lily called, hurrying after her. "Listen to this!"

"Lily! You're up early," Lympia said over her shoulder. She weaved into the laundry room, unsteady under the weight of the tablecloths. "Any reason?"

"Well," said Lily, "let's just say I may have an invention as good as your laundry cleaner!" She plunked her bottle of panglory seeds down onto a laundry-sorting table. "These little seeds are going to become some amazing flowers! I'm calling them panglories."

"That's great, Lily!" Lympia said. Her eyes went to a row of sea-glass bottles on a nearby shelf. She picked one up, a sly smile on her face. "But will they work as well as my cleaner?" she teased.

Lympia uncorked the bottle. She poured a few small, brown pebbles into her hand. They didn't look like much. But Lily knew these were the miracle cleaner that Lympia had made.

"We've been trying it on everything." Lympia put the bottle down on the table. She reached for a pile of clean, folded laundry. "Have you ever seen spider lace look whiter?" Lympia asked.

Lily had to admit the linens looked brand-new. They gleamed in the sunshine that streamed in through the laundry room windows. The piles of clean laundry stacked on the tables all looked like new—maybe better.

*Lympia's invention may be the best of all*, Lily thought. No longer would the fairies have to worry about spilling raspberry juice on tablecloths and dribbling strawberry shortcake down shirtfronts.

"Okay, okay," Lily said. "My seeds aren't as well tested as your laundry cleaner . . . yet." She smiled and picked up the bottle from the table. "But if these little things work . . . well, hang on to your clothespins!"

AFTER LILY HAD TALKED to Lympia, she'd run into Silvermist by the court-yard. Then she had grabbed a bite to eat from the kitchen. Almost two hours had passed before she headed for her garden.

When Lily got there, she could hardly believe her eyes. When she had left the garden early in the morning, her patch of sandy soil had been bare. But *now*—now a thick blanket of tiny purple, yellow, and pink panglories covered every inch of the patch! Even seeds that had fallen on the bark and the acorns around the spot had sprouted. She'd never imagined that her little seeds would bloom so quickly.

Lily had done it! She'd created a whole new kind of flower. The seeds had grown almost exactly as she'd expected them to. Except for one detail—the panglories sprouted anywhere and everywhere! In the soil, yes, but on bark and on acorns, too.

Slowly, another thought came to Lily. She could make all of Pixie Hollow more beautiful with these seeds. She imagined panglories growing on fences, tree trunks . . . even rocks!

"Bumble! Bumble!" Lily called out. She spotted her friend buzzing around a honeysuckle flower and waved him over. "Come look!"

Bumble dove into the panglories. He was very impressed—or maybe he just wanted to grab some nectar from Lily's newest flowers.

"My little seeds!" Lily dropped to her knees by the panglory patch and gathered the flowers into a hug. "You're all grown up! You've done so well!" She thought she might actually burst with pride. She felt like shouting the news from the top of the Home Tree. She couldn't wait to tell the other garden fairies!

Just then, Iris flew past the far end of Lily's garden. "Lily!" she called out from the other side of the gate. "I just heard! The Lonely Heart flower near the well is about to *double*-bloom!"

"Iris!" Lily called back. "I'm so glad you're here. Come see my pangl—"

But Iris had already rushed off. Lily couldn't blame her. The Lonely Heart was one of the rarest flowers in Pixie Hollow. Its single pink and gold flower bloomed for only five days out of the whole year. But every once in a while, a Lonely Heart sprouted two blooms at once! Not many garden fairies had been in Never Land long enough to remember the last time that had happened.

Lily felt torn. She looked at her

panglories. Then she looked where Iris had flown. She didn't want to miss seeing the Lonely Heart double-bloom. But she wanted to stay with her panglories, too.

Finally, she shook her wings and flew toward the well. The double-bloom happened so rarely. Besides, the panglories would be waiting for her when she got back to her garden.

"Bumble!" she called over her shoulder. "Want to come?"

Lily heard her friend buzzing along behind her to catch up. She checked to make sure her bottle of seeds was still in her pocket. There would be lots of garden fairies at the well. She could tell them all about her invention!

Lily and Bumble caught up with Iris

near the well. Rosetta, Bluebell, Fern, Aster, and several other garden talents were waiting there. They hovered around a tall, green stalk topped with two still-closed blooms. Bumble buzzed ahead, pausing in front of each bloom. Then he came to rest on a daisy next to Lily.

"Iris! Lily!" Rosetta called. "You haven't missed anything. But it looks like the blooms will open any moment now."

"Well," Lily began, "I have some news while we wait. Actually, it's about an invention!"

She described the seeds she had mixed. She told the other fairies what she had done that morning. Then she pulled the seeds from her pocket. Bumble buzzed cheerfully around the bottle. It was almost as if he was trying to help Lily show the seeds off.

"They grew on acorns?" Aster cried in disbelief.

"And *bark*?" Rosetta said.

Lily nodded. "I'm hoping they'll grow on *anything*! Watch!" She put the bottle down on the edge of the well and uncorked it. "I bet they'll sprout on the stones of the well."

The fairies clustered around Lily to watch. Not wanting to be left out, Bumble squeezed himself between Aster and Bluebell. For a second, his wing got snagged on Aster's belt. He tugged away, trying to free himself. Then, suddenly, he came loose and rocketed forward. He tumbled in midair and crashed into the sea-glass bottle full of seeds.

"Look out!" Lily cried. She lunged forward, trying to catch the bottle.

But the glass slipped through her fingers. A loud splash echoed far below.

Lily stared into the dark well in disbelief. She could just make out the base of the bottle as it sank into the water.

Bumble landed on the edge of the well next to Lily. He let out a quiet droning moan.

"Oh, Bumble, I know you didn't mean to," Lily said. She patted her friend on his fuzzy back. "It's all right. I can make more."

But could she? All the seeds she had worked on were inside that bottle. And

she hadn't written down the formula she'd used to make them. She wasn't sure she'd be able to remember just how she had done it.

Lily tried to stay cheerful. "I guess my wing-tingling panglory show will have to wait until I can make more seeds," she said to the others.

"It'll be just as good then, Lily," Rosetta said.

"Oh, look, look!" Iris suddenly cried. She was pointing at the Lonely Heart. "Something's happening!"

Sure enough, both blossoms were slowly opening at the same time. The pink petals unfolded first to reveal golden blooms inside. It looked like a fiery sunset inside the flower's bloom. It was a breathtaking sight. Lily was glad she hadn't missed it.

And yet, if she had stayed in her garden, she'd still have her panglory seeds.

5

FOR THE THIRD MORNING in a row, Lily skipped breakfast. There was too much to be done in her garden to spend time chatting in the tearoom.

Lily was mixing another batch of panglories. She'd had no luck with the second and third batches. Something was still missing.

Her stomach rumbled as the sun hid behind gray clouds. A little rain right about now would save her some trips to the well. Getting enough water for the seeds had meant many flights back and forth.

Lily's other plants were also thirsty. Morning glories, poppies, lilies of the valley, violets—even some larkspur and sweet peas. She had hardly given her garden a thought, so she spent the rest of the morning taking care of it. She hoped a break from the panglories would help her remember what she was missing.

She weeded and watered. She put up a striped pole for the vining plants to climb onto. She pulled dried leaves off stems and spread plant food all over.

Bumble followed along behind her, nosing his head into the blooms.

Lily was cheering on her sweet peas when Rosetta landed at her side. In one hand she held a little package wrapped in leaf paper. Her other hand rested on her hip.

"Lily! You've got to eat!" Rosetta scolded. "I know you've been working hard, but this is silly! I haven't seen you at breakfast for days!"

"I know, Rosetta," Lily replied. "It's just—"

"Yes, yes," Rosetta said knowingly. "With those new seeds of yours, you're running yourself ragged." She opened the leaf-paper package. Inside were two thick slices of red currant bread. She handed them to Lily. "I thought you might want these."

Lily took the bread eagerly. "It's 'ood, 'osetta," she mumbled, her mouth full. She gobbled both slices and washed them down with a ladleful of fresh water. "Much better," she said with a sigh.

"I'm glad," Rosetta said. She threw

an arm around her friend. "I'm almost afraid to ask. But . . . how is it going?"

Lily's shoulders slumped. "It hasn't been easy," she said. "Well, maybe I should just show you."

Lily flew over to a mossy area under a maple tree. A bunch of seeds sat on the moss. "My second batch never took root," she explained.

Farther ahead, Lily pointed out a patch of scraggly, overgrown flowers. "The third batch is a little too eager. They didn't stop growing. I might have gone a little heavy on the pepper with that batch," she said.

"As for the fourth batch . . ." Lily flew around to the side of her garden shed. Rosetta followed—and stopped in

midair. Her mouth hung open. Lily hid a
giggle behind her hand.

The side of the shed was covered in
small, colorful panglories—from corner
to corner and top to bottom. It was as if
someone had draped the shed with a
floral blanket. Tall trees shaded the shed.
It was one of the darkest spots in Lily's
garden. Even so, the bright purple, yellow,
and pink flowers bloomed cheerfully.
They seemed perfectly happy with their
quiet, shady little corner.

Rosetta studied the way the flowers
had rooted themselves right into the
wooden shingles. Then she swung toward
Lily, amazed. "This batch—"

"—turned out just right," Lily
finished for her. She was wearing a huge

grin. "And this time, I wrote down *exactly* how I made them!"

"Lily!" Rosetta exclaimed at last. "This is incredible! Can you imagine what we can do with seeds like this?"

Lily nodded excitedly.

"How did you . . . ? I mean, what can they . . . ?" Rosetta stopped herself. She took a deep breath before going on. "I have a million questions. But the *first* thing I want to know is . . ."

"Yes?" Lily asked.

Rosetta flew to Lily's side. She clasped her hands and smiled her sweetest smile. She batted her eyelashes. Finally, she asked, "When can *I* get some of these seeds?"

# 6

LILY TRIED TO TELL ROSETTA that the seeds weren't ready to be passed around. Of course she wanted to see them put to good use. But for now, she didn't feel comfortable letting them go.

Rosetta, however, was very convincing. In the end, Lily agreed that Rosetta could hand out some of the seeds, but only to other garden talents. They could test them in their gardens. If there were any problems, they could tell Lily before she gave the seeds to the other talents. Lily didn't want all the fairies to get excited and then find out the seeds didn't work as she'd said they would.

But by the end of the afternoon, there didn't seem to be much chance of that happening.

Lily herself had spent the day trying the seeds all over her garden. She threw a handful on a hollow log. She sprinkled some on two lanterns that were hanging near the front gate. She tossed seeds on a wicker garden basket, on a plant label, and even on the backs of her gardening gloves. Wherever she tried the panglory seeds, they sprouted—and quickly!

Lily was eager to find out if any of the other garden talents had tried the seeds. She flew off to see the results.

"Lily!" Aster cried. She stood up from her gardening when she saw Lily. "These seeds of yours are amazing!"

Lily glanced around Aster's garden. She spotted the panglories. Then she realized they were covering the metal garden tools Aster was working with!

"Can I get some more?" Aster asked hopefully.

Bluebell's garden was full of the little flowers, too. All her stepping stones were covered in colorful panglories. "They're almost too pretty to step on now, aren't they?" Bluebell said to Lily.

On her way to Rosetta's garden, Lily found Iris watering the thick roots of the Home Tree. It was a chore the garden fairies took turns doing. Lily hadn't seen Iris do it for ages.

"You know I don't do much gardening anymore," Iris said. She had once told Lily that growing things just didn't come naturally to her, even though she loved plants and flowers. "But these flowers, Lily . . ." Iris pulled her plant book from her bag. It was covered in cheerful blooms. Iris smiled proudly. "Even *I* can grow these!" she exclaimed.

Lily beamed. It was great that the seeds worked so well. But it was even better that Iris was excited about gardening again.

At last, Lily reached Rosetta's garden. Rosetta flew to meet her at the front gate. She grabbed Lily's hand and pulled her in.

"You've got to see this!" Rosetta told her. She led Lily to an out-of-the-way corner of her garden. Rosetta pulled back a curtain of climbing roses. Behind it was a small pond—a favorite quiet spot of Rosetta's.

Lily gasped. All over the surface were flowering panglories!

"They really do grow *anywhere!*" Rosetta cried.

Lily sighed with happiness. Her invention was a success! She finally felt ready to share her panglories with all of Pixie Hollow.

That evening at dinner, each table had a special floral decoration in the center.

The garden fairies got to the tearoom early. They sat at their table, trying to stay calm. But they were giggling with anticipation. They couldn't wait to see everyone's reaction!

Slowly, the tearoom filled up with hungry fairies and sparrow men.

"What in Never Land is it?" Lily heard Fira say at the light-talent table.

"How does it work?" Silvermist asked at the water-talent table. "Are those flowers really—"

"—growing out of that rock?" Rani finished for her.

At the animal-talent table, Fawn was holding up the decoration. She studied the bottom. She looked very confused.

Tink was the first one to come over to the garden fairies. She was carrying the centerpiece from the pots-and-pans talents' table. It was a stone about the size of a fairy's hand, with purple, yellow, and pink panglories growing on the top.

"I don't suppose," Tink began, "any of you know anything about these?"

Aster covered up a giggle. Bluebell tried not to smile. Lily looked at Rosetta, who was biting her lip to keep from laughing. They couldn't hold it in any longer. Everyone at the table burst into laughter.

Finally, Lily recovered enough to

answer. "Yes," she said. "We made
them!" She felt proud from her wingtips
to her toes.

"They're Lily's amazing new invention!" Rosetta added.

"They're called panglories," Aster
put in. "And they'll grow *anywhere!*"

Tink looked skeptical. "Really?" she
asked. "Anywhere?"

Lily opened her mouth to reply. But Fern beat her to it. "Uh-huh," Fern said. "They grew on my wheelbarrow."

"And my gardening book!" said Iris.

"And my pond!" cried Rosetta.

The garden fairies went on and on. Meanwhile, something on Tink's bunch of flowers caught Lily's eye. She leaned in for a closer look.

*Huh, that's funny,* Lily thought. Two or three of the flowers had faded leaves on their stems. So far, all the panglories from the fourth batch of seeds had been perfect in every way. Their color was perfect. Their shape was perfect. They were perfectly healthy.

She shrugged it off. *Maybe these just need a bit more water,* she decided. Then she turned her attention back to Tink and the garden fairies.

"You know, Tink," Rosetta teased, "I think the garden-talent fairies have something special here. We can't wait to see what you come up with!" She knew Tink hadn't meant to extend the challenge the way she had—putting down the other talents' important jobs. But if any fairy could put a challenge to good use, Tinker Bell was the one to do it.

Tink smiled and turned to go. "It'll knock your sun hats off!" she said as she flew away.

It could have just been Lily's imagination . . . but didn't Tink look a tiny bit worried?

## 7

WHEN LILY OPENED HER EYES the next morning, the panglories were the first thing she saw. She had carried home a bunch of decorations the night before. The other fairies had been so impressed! Even Queen Clarion had given the flowers a second look. Lily's glow had flared with pride.

She bent low over a centerpiece. "Well done!" she said to the flowers.

Then she caught a glimpse of something among the leaves. Was this the same bunch that had faded leaves the night before?

Lily studied them more closely. Several leaves were looking worse than faded—they looked downright gray. She checked the other centerpieces. Nearly all of them had at least a couple of faded leaves. On the worst ones, entire stems were spotted gray.

Lily sat in her desk chair and looked out the window toward her garden. She felt an urge to check the panglories there. It probably wasn't a big deal. Maybe it was how these seeds had been planted.

Or maybe the flowers didn't like being indoors or planted in rocks. All the same, she wanted to look them over, just to make sure.

In her garden, Lily zipped from one patch of panglories to another. She started with the first ones she'd planted in the sandy soil. She ended up at the fourth batch growing on the shed. Each time she stopped, her heart sank a little bit more. All the panglories in the garden were as gray as the ones in the center-pieces. If anything, her garden panglories seemed worse.

Lily fretted over the plants. Were they sick? But nothing else about them had changed. That was the funny thing. None of them looked droopy or wilted.

They were all just very, *very* pale.

Bumble buzzed over to Lily from a poppy he'd been nestled in. Lily looked at her friend and then back at the flowers. "What's going on?" she muttered. "What happened to all the bright colors?"

Lily sighed. For just a moment, she slumped against the gate. Everything had been going so well! But she didn't let herself feel down for long. She straightened up and turned to the nearest panglory patch. "Well, we'll figure it out. You'll have your color back in no time!" she said cheerfully.

For the rest of the day, Lily took care of the panglories. She sprinkled them with big pinches of fairy dust. She tickled them under their petals. She even

watered them an extra time before heading home for the evening.

The next morning, Lily entered the garden feeling hopeful. But when she saw the panglories, she stopped short. "Oh, no!" she cried.

The flowers were no better. In fact, many looked faded right through the petals.

Lily spent the whole day in her

garden. She was so worried about her flowers, she no longer cared about Tink's challenge. She just wanted to see the colorful blossoms growing strong again. She watered. She tended. She weeded. She even asked a light-talent fairy to shine some extra light on the pansies.

"Let's hope this works," she said to Bumble as the sun was setting.

Despite all her hard work, the flowers were no better the next day. Now entire patches of panglories were gray. There was no sign of the bright shades of purple, yellow, or pink they'd once had.

Lily hovered in the middle of her garden. She looked around. She hated to say it. She hated to even think it. She loved all plants—even the bossiest weeds. But her panglories were becoming a problem.

Even so, Lily never thought about giving up on them. She flew to Rosetta's garden for advice. She found her friend tending a bed of young snapdragons.

"Rosetta, I have a question for you. Are your panglories having any problems?" Lily asked.

"Oh," replied Rosetta. "You mean the color loss?"

Lily was taken aback by Rosetta's candid remark. Rosetta took her arm. "Here, I'll show you," she said.

She led Lily to her pond. All the panglories floating on it were different shades of gray. Some of them looked almost white.

Lily gasped. "Yours too?"

Rosetta nodded. Lily could see pity in her eyes. "And Aster's and Bluebell's and Fern's and Iris's," Rosetta added.

"What?" Lily cried. "Since when? Why didn't you tell me?"

"It's been happening slowly. I guess it started a couple of days ago," said Rosetta. "No one had the heart to tell you. We thought maybe yours were still doing well. We didn't want to worry you."

Lily buried her head in her hands. Disappointment washed over her like a wave.

Rosetta touched Lily's arm. "Don't worry, Lily," she said. "We'll figure out what went wrong. Maybe we can fix it."

Lily looked up and forced a smile. "I don't care about the invention challenge. But I've spent a lot of time with those flowers now," she said.

"You care about them," Rosetta said.

Lily nodded. "I want them to be happy and healthy. And they seemed to be working so well. But without their color . . ." Lily sighed. "Maybe I need a break from the panglories. I've barely taken care of my other plants. I guess they could use more attention."

Rosetta promised to drop in on Lily later. Then she went back to her garden.

Lily was halfway to the front gate when she heard Rosetta gasp. Lily turned.

Rosetta was staring at a snapdragon in disbelief. "Lily, look!" she cried.

Lily flew over. "Is it just me," Rosetta said, "or do these leaves look like—"

"The fading leaves on the pan-glories!" Lily cried. "It can't be." She shook her head.

Rosetta gasped again. Now she was looking at some irises. "Look! Here, too!" she cried. Sure enough, the bottom halves of the stalks were strangely gray.

"And here," said Lily. She had noticed a few buttercups, colorless up to their petals. "Oh, no," she moaned. "What's going on?"

There was only one explanation. But Lily forced it out of her mind. She didn't want to think about it—not until she checked the other gardens.

Lily stopped off at each of the other

garden fairies' gardens. What she found was not good. She grew more and more concerned with each visit.

Fern was crazy with worry over her lavender plants. She had found grayish spots on their stems that morning.

Aster's weeping willows looked very pale. Aster wasn't looking much better herself.

Bluebell's ivy plants were still climbing nicely. But it looked like the lower halves of the vines had been drained of all color.

And back in her own garden, Lily found many flowers that showed signs of fading.

Lily plopped down on a tree stump. She put her head in her hands. Her panglories weren't perfect. And now it seemed that the rest of the garden plants might have the same problem.

Whatever was wrong with the panglories, could it be . . . contagious?

# 8

K*NOCK*, *KNOCK*.

Inside her garden shed, Lily jumped at the noise. She sat in the center of a circle of gray flowers. She'd been studying them for hours, but she still had no idea what was wrong with them.

The knock came again. Lily opened the door and poked her head out.

Standing there were Scarlett and Azure, two art-talent fairies.

"We know you're hard at work," said Azure. "Rosetta told me you're figuring out what's wrong with the flowers."

Lily guessed that word had spread. It had been two days since she'd first seen the fading leaves on the other plants.

Scarlett cleared her throat. "It's just that . . . well, we're all out of orange paint," she said. "We were wondering if you had any orange flowers."

"So we could make more paint," Azure added.

Lily stepped out of the shed. She looked around her garden and winced. It already seemed much worse than when she had left it just a few hours before.

Most of Lily's garden looked like a black-and-white copy of itself. In a few places, there were hints of pale green, washed-out pink, and light lavender. But there was no sign of orange.

Lily shrugged at the art-talent fairies. "All I have is what you see," she said. "Are you sure you're completely out?"

Azure nodded. "We haven't gotten any new flowers for days," she said.

Lily sighed. Without the colorful flowers from Pixie Hollow's gardens, the art talents couldn't make their paint.

"Have you tried the other garden fairies?" Lily asked hopefully.

"Yes, but their gardens all look pretty much like yours," Scarlett said.

Lily's wings drooped. Was it her

fault? That was all she could think about since Rosetta had noticed the faded leaves on her snapdragon. Before she'd invented the panglories, all the other plants had been healthy. The panglories had been the first plants to lose their color. And now, days later, the rest of the garden had faded, too. There had to be a connection.

And it wasn't just the garden fairies' problem anymore. Scarlett and Azure's visit proved that. The color loss was also hurting the other talents.

Suddenly, Lily lost her temper. Her glow flashed bright orange and she stomped her foot. "I wish I'd never made those seeds!" she cried.

Scarlett and Azure looked surprised.

They had never seen Lily so upset before. Normally, she was one of the calmest fairies in Pixie Hollow.

"Don't worry, Lily," Scarlett said. "It will be okay."

Just as quickly as it had flared up, Lily's temper died down. Another thought replaced it. This one sent a cold trickle of dread through her wings. She hadn't known about the art talents running out of paint. Could other talents be having trouble, too?

There was only one way to find out. She hated to leave her sick flowers for even a second, but she needed to take a quick tour around Pixie Hollow.

"I'll get you some orange flowers as soon as I figure out what happened,"

Lily said to Scarlett and Azure. Then she flew off to see what other problems the panglories might have caused.

Lily began outside the Home Tree. She peeked through the kitchen window. The baking fairies were busy making cupcakes.

"What?" Dulcie was saying. "We're

out of colored icing? We can't just make white cupcakes with plain white icing! That's not very pretty!"

*Oh, no!* Lily pulled away from the window. Of course the baking talents would be out of dyes, too. The sick feeling of dread had moved to her stomach. She steeled herself to go on.

Lily flew around the Home Tree to a tearoom window. She watched the decorating fairies set up for that evening's dinner. They looked unhappy as they put white and gray flowers into vases.

"It's not very colorful," one of them said. "But it'll have to do. These are the brightest blooms Rosetta had."

Two floors up, things weren't any better in the sewing room. Through the window, Lily saw a couple of fairies piecing together a flower-petal dress.

"I guess the fashionable color this season will be gray," Tack said.

Taylor laughed. "It's not like we have any other choice!"

With a choked sob, Lily turned away. Everyone was making the best of it. No one was blaming her. But what was Pixie Hollow without bright flowers? No pretty dresses. No colorful tarts and cakes. No beautifully painted pictures or pottery.

Lily made herself fly on. She had to see how bad it really was with the art talents. At their sunny studio, the art fairies were trying hard to get by. Using dried flowers, they had made more paint.

But Bess, for one, wasn't pleased with it. "Dried flowers just aren't as good as fresh ones," she said. She stepped back from her easel. "These colors are washed out."

Lily's heart felt heavy. She found a quiet spot on a top branch of the Home Tree. She sat down there, her elbows on her knees and her head in her hands.

She could see most of Pixie Hollow from here. Her eyes were drawn to the pockets of gray below. She knew some of them were the garden fairies' nearly colorless gardens.

"How did this happen?" Lily asked herself. "I was trying to make Pixie Hollow more beautiful, not less!" So many fairies were worse off because of

her mistake. But she didn't know how to fix the problem.

Something fluttered in the breeze close by and caught Lily's eye. She turned to it—and froze. It couldn't possibly be what she thought it was.

Lily flew out to the end of the branch. She hovered over the leaves that had gotten her attention. Then she flew a little bit higher to get a better view. She tried telling herself they looked yellow or brown—anything but gray. But the closer she looked, the clearer it became.

Not the Home Tree! Not the most important plant in all of Pixie Hollow. But there was no way to deny it.

The Home Tree was losing its color, too.

## 9

Lily rocketed away from the top branch
of the graying Home Tree. It was time to
ask for help—before *all* of Pixie Hollow
turned gray! She knew the first fairy she
needed to go to.

She flew past the courtyard and
through the hallways of the Home Tree,
until she came to a door.

She knocked and the door opened.

"I need to see the queen," Lily said breathlessly.

Rhia, the queen's helper, let Lily in. Within moments Lily was sitting with the queen, pouring her heart out. Queen Clarion and Lily talked for more than an hour. No one ever knew what they had discussed, but that evening, just after dinner, Queen Clarion asked all the fairies to gather in the courtyard.

Everyone filed outside, mumbling. Lily felt many eyes upon her. Her glow turned pink with embarrassment under their stares. But nothing could make her feel any worse than she already did.

When all the fairies were outside, the queen called for quiet.

"I'm sure many of you are aware of what's been happening," Queen Clarion began. "The flowers have been losing their color. No one knows why."

The queen turned to Lily, who was standing at her side. "Lily wants to talk to all of you about this problem. Maybe together we can figure out what's gone wrong."

Queen Clarion gave Lily a quick, encouraging nod.

Lily took a deep breath. A knot tightened in her stomach. All the fairies and sparrow men were staring at her.

She closed her eyes and tried not to think about how she had let everyone down. When she opened them again, she told everyone about the panglories as quickly as she could. She started with her original idea for the seeds and explained everything that had happened, including how the other plants had faded as well.

Then it was time for the really hard part. Lily looked up at the sky. She couldn't meet anyone's stare.

"B-b-b-but I've got even more bad news," she went on. She almost choked on the words.

She took another deep breath. She could feel tears filling the corners of her eyes. "Now it looks like the Home Tree is fading, too," she said.

Cries of alarm rippled through the crowd. Lily's head sank low.

The Home Tree wasn't just the fairies' home. It was the center of their world. It was the heart and soul of Pixie Hollow.

Lily just had to add one more thing. "I've been working to figure out what's going on," she called over the murmurs of worry and confusion. "I wish I could say that I know what the problem is. But I don't. If any of you have any ideas . . ." She trailed off.

The crowd fell silent.

Lily flew quickly to a pebble and sat down. She wished someone would say something—*anything*. She'd rather hear what the other fairies were thinking, even if it wasn't good.

Suddenly, a loud *clatter, clatter, clank!* broke the silence.

All eyes turned toward the noise. Fairies on one side of the courtyard looked behind them and moved aside to make room for Lympia and Breeze, another laundry-talent fairy. They were carrying a big metal washtub between them.

They landed awkwardly in the center of the courtyard and dropped the washtub with another clank. Both fairies were out of breath.

"Queen Clarion," panted Lympia, "we didn't mean to be late."

"That's all right, Lympia," Queen Clarion said. "It looks as though something slowed you down."

"What?" said Lympia. Then she realized the queen meant the washtub. "Oh, yes, there's that," she said. "But also, we were in the laundry room. And we . . . we have something to show everyone." Lympia seemed excited. Breeze, too, was having trouble hovering in just one spot.

The two fairies bent over the washtub. "We were washing this blanket,"

said Lympia. "All we used was water and some of my new laundry cleaner. And an amazing thing happened."

Lympia and Breeze straightened up. They opened a dripping-wet blanket. Lympia held one corner and Breeze another.

A few gasps were heard throughout the crowd as all the fairies stared at the blanket.

There was something on the blanket. It looked like . . . like half the blanket was covered in little pansies!

## 10

"Oooh!" A cry went up from the fairies around the courtyard.

"Look at that bright purple," Bess whispered to the other art talents.

Many fairies were delighted to see flowers growing on a blanket. A few clapped. But some of them—especially the garden fairies—looked confused.

Lily was the most confused garden talent of all. She knew what those flowers were. They were her panglories!

Lily flew to the front of the crowd. "Lympia, where did you get panglory seeds?" she asked.

Lympia shook her head. "No, Lily. It wasn't your seeds," she said. She held up a sea-glass bottle. "They grew from my laundry cleaner! I just opened this new bottle this morning."

She turned to look at the queen. "I don't know how it happened. But it seems my cleaner can get out stains *and* it can grow flowers on laundry!"

Lily took a corner of the blanket in her hands and carefully looked at the flowers. The bright purple, yellow, and pink blooms sprouted from the cloth. They looked as beautiful as they had that first day in Lily's garden.

"These look just like panglories," Lily said. "Are you sure you didn't sprinkle panglory seeds on the wash instead of cleaner? We did hand out a lot of seeds. Maybe one of the other garden talents left some in a pocket or something." Lily looked around hopefully at her friends. That had to be it! How else would her special panglory seeds have ended up in the laundry?

But the other garden talents just shrugged. They all seemed as puzzled as Lily did. No one had seen such brilliant flowers in days.

"I didn't wash any clothes with this

blanket," Lympia told her. "And I took this bottle from my shelf of detergent bottles."

Doubt flickered in Lily's mind for a moment. She was sure the flowers were her panglories. But Lympia had a point. How would panglory seeds have gotten mixed in with the blanket?

While the other fairies pressed in closer to Lympia and Breeze, Lily backed away. She tried to remember every detail from when she'd invented the panglories. She knew she hadn't even seen Lympia since the day she'd planted that first batch of panglory seeds.

Lily sighed, remembering the excitement of that morning. It seemed like such a long time ago now. She had just tried out the seeds. She'd been eager to learn what would happen. She'd flown around Pixie Hollow as she waited to see how her flowers would bloom.

*Wait!* thought Lily. *I had the seed bottle in my pocket at the time. . . .*

A sea-glass seed bottle! Lily's memories rushed back to her. She *had* shown Lympia the seeds! She had put them on the folding table. Then Lympia had shown her the laundry cleaner.

Why, that would explain everything!

Lily flew to the queen's side. "Queen Clarion! I know what's going on!" she cried. The loudness of her voice shocked even her. "I can explain it all!"

A look of surprise passed over the queen's face. It matched the look on the faces all around the courtyard. The rest of the fairies fell silent.

Lily felt everyone's eyes on her again. But this time she didn't mind at all.

"I was excited after I planted my flowers. I couldn't wait to tell someone. I found Lympia doing the wash in the Home Tree. Do you remember, Lympia?" Lily looked at her hopefully. "I had my bottle of seeds with me. It looked a lot like the one your cleaner is in."

Lympia nodded slowly. Then she gasped. "Lily . . . do you think? Could the bottles—"

"Yes!" Lily agreed. Lympia remembered her visit, and now Lympia was thinking the same thing she was!

Lympia handed her corner of the

blanket to Breeze. Then she held her sea-glass bottle up to her eyes. She wrinkled her brow. Lily knew what she was thinking. The brown stones inside the bottle looked like cleaning pebbles. But they could be seeds, too.

Lympia held the bottle out to Lily. Lily's wings fluttered as she took the sea-glass bottle. She was nervous and excited and hopeful.

She tipped the bottle over her hand. Some of the pebbles fell into her palm. If she had to guess, she would say that the pebbles were actually her seeds. But there was only one way to know for sure.

Lily kneeled beside the washtub. She looked up at the crowd of fairies around her. "Here goes," she said. She spread the handful of pebbles out on the ground.

Panglories were unique in many ways. But they didn't bloom any more quickly than normal flowers. Lily knew they would need extra-special help. She usually didn't demand so much of her flowers. But this was important. Maybe they would sprout quickly for her, if she asked.

Lily leaned in close and whispered, "If you're my seeds, grow strong. I believe in you."

She could feel the crowd waiting. Queen Clarion hovered right beside her as everyone looked to see if the brown stones were cleaning pebbles or panglory seeds.

Nothing happened. Could Lily have

been wrong? Had it just been a bottle of Lympia's cleaner after all? She shut her eyes tightly. She thought about her color-less garden. She remembered the art and baking talents' problems. She recalled the Home Tree's graying leaves.

"I know you can do it," she whispered to the seeds. "You can do so much already. Sprout. Flower. Show your beautiful blossoms to Pixie Hollow."

Lily heard the queen gasp. She opened her eyes and looked at the ground. There, blooming in the middle of the courtyard, were lovely purple, yellow, and pink panglories. The other fairies began to cheer.

Lily sighed happily.

Queen Clarion cleared her throat. "We now know what happened to your seeds, Lily. But we still don't know why the other flowers in Pixie Hollow, and the Home Tree, are gray."

"Oh, right," said Lily. There was more to explain. She told everyone how she'd left the laundry room that morning. She had flown back to her garden. She had found her panglory seeds already blooming. And then she had flown to the well with Bumble to see the Lonely Heart flower double-bloom.

"I still had the bottle of seeds," Lily said. "At least, I *thought* it was a bottle of seeds. I was going to show the other garden fairies how well the seeds bloomed—on anything!"

"That's right!" Rosetta said from across the courtyard. "And Bumble knocked the bottle into the well."

Next to Rosetta, Iris scratched her head. "But if it wasn't a bottle of seeds—"

Lily finished her thought. "—then it

was a bottle of Lympia's cleaner that went down the well. Splash! Right into our well water." She paused to see if anyone understood. "It's the well water that we use to water our gardens."

One by one, the faces of the garden fairies brightened. Most of the other talents still looked confused. But garden fairies knew how plants worked.

"And when we watered our plants—" Bluebell started.

"—we whitened all the flowers!" Aster finished.

The garden-talent fairies looked at each other and burst out laughing. Even Queen Clarion smiled about the mix-up.

"Lily, your panglories were just the first flowers to start fading. They weren't the cause of any of it!" Rosetta cried.

Lily beamed.

"But why would the Home Tree fade?" Queen Clarion asked.

"Because of me," Iris and Fern said at the exact same time. "What? You?" the two fairies cried, looking at each other.

"Yes, me," Iris went on. "I watered the Home Tree roots a few days ago— with water from the well." She explained that it was something the garden fairies took turns doing.

"I did, too," said Fern. "Iris, you haven't watered the Home Tree in ages! I've taken your spot in the watering schedule."

So the Home Tree had gotten a double dose of Lympia's laundry cleaner.

That explained its graying leaves.

"Mystery solved," Queen Clarion said. "We'll have our colorful gardens back in no time!"

The crowd cheered once more. As they started to fly off, Lily trailed behind the rest. She couldn't wait to get back to tending her garden! Once the water-talent fairies cleaned the well, Lily would have orange flowers for the art talents again. She'd have pink and yellow and blue flowers so the baking talents could make colorful icing. And she'd have a fresh batch of panglories sprouting from the patch in her garden where other flowers refused to grow.

A couple of days later, Lily was lying on a mound of soft moss in her garden. At her side, a patch of colorful panglories sprouted on a frog-shaped garden statue.

Lily closed her eyes and smiled. All was fine in Pixie Hollow. The garden and water fairies had rinsed out the well. And just as she had hoped, the color had come back to the gardens. The Home Tree no longer showed any sign of fading. And Lily's panglories were blooming in every spare inch of her garden, everywhere her regular plants couldn't.

Lily's garden looked better—and happier—than ever. All she wanted now was to sit back and enjoy it.

"Lily!" a voice cried from the garden gate. Lily looked over. It was Rosetta.

Tink hovered at her side. Lily flew over to meet them.

"Do you like my new dress?" Rosetta asked. "It's the latest in fairy fashion." She twirled around. Her dress was covered in pink panglories. "The dress-making fairies are having a lot of fun with your invention."

"I guess I was wrong, Lily," Tink said. "We all think up great ideas for our talents."

She pulled a flowery hat from behind her back and put it on Rosetta's head. It was the firefly-headlamp hat, covered in panglories!

Lily laughed out loud. Tink's great invention looked pretty silly covered in flowers! "That's one fairy fashion I hope

doesn't catch on," Lily said. "Me, I'll stick to my regular sun hat . . . and to my regular talent."

Lily had loved the thrill of making something no one had ever seen before. And maybe someday she would want to try creating something new again. But for now, she was content to feel the sun on her face, the grass between her toes, and the breeze on her wings.

# Coming soon from PAPERCUTZ™

### Graphic Novel #1
## "PRILLA'S TALENT"

Travel to Never Land with Tinker Bell, Prilla and your favorite Fairies in this full-color graphic novel from Papercutz. Featuring four comicbook stories you won't soon forget!

5 x 7½, 80 pages, full-color,
$7.99/$9.99 CAN
ISBN: 978-1-59707-186-4
Also Available in hardcover!

# Imagine If You Caught A Fairy...

## WALT DISNEY
### PICTURES

# TinkerBell
### AND THE
# GREAT FAIRY RESCUE

## All-New Movie On Blu-ray™ Combo Pack & DVD Coming Soon

Visit DisneyFairies.com